Daddy Likes to Dance

By Amanda J Smith

Daddy likes to Dance

Contact: mjsmith0778@gmail.com
Illustrator: Gonmuki
Interior Design: hDigitals Design Studio

ISBN   978-0-57895-748-7 (Hardback)
ISBN   978-0-57895-749-4 (eBook)

To my husband Michael, the most amazing father to our girls. Thank you for continually making JoJo and Teddy smile.

Do you have a daddy that's silly like mine?

He dances and twirls around all the time.

My mommy just laughs at him and shakes her head.

He grabs her by her hands
and spins her instead.

He wiggles and jiggles and makes funny faces.

He'll bust a move in the silliest places

He sticks out his tongue and
boops me on the nose

He makes me giggle by tickling my toes

He's not the best dancer,
he says that is me

He loves when I twirl, I giggle with glee

Sometimes when I'm naughty
or a grumpy bear

He lifts me up and spins me in the air

My daddy plays dolls with me
and sits to have tea

He tries really hard to be pretty like me

Just when I think he is too tired for fun

He puts down his work and says,
you better run!

He likes to play board games;
I always go first

He's not very good,
but he isn't the worst

There's no one I'd rather be with than my silly dad.

The thing I look forward to when I go to bed
Is a dance party boogie then a kiss on my head

I hope that your daddy is silly too.
My daddy is. Daddy, I love you.

CPSIA information can be obtained
at www.ICGtesting.com
Printed in the USA
BVRC102115300821
615622BV00007BA/126